Understanding Your Mate

To: Carronée

O(t what a change

Now Enjoy the Goodness of the Lord

Antonio Harlan

Southfield, Michigan

Understanding Your Mate
by Rev. Antonio Harlan
Copyright 2008
AMZA Publishing
16250 Northland Dr., Suite 210
Southfield, MI 48075
313-632-6527
www.understandingyourmate.com
amza@comcast.net

Interior Layout:
Selah Branding and Design LLC
www.selahbrandinganddesign.com

Edited By: Tracey Vasil Biscontini
Northeast Editing, Inc.
82 William Street
Pittston, PA 18640
v. 570-602-1538
f. 570-602-1575
http://www.ne-edit.com

Publisher: AMZA Publishing (2008)

ISBN-10: 0981752721
ISBN-13: 978-0981752723

ASIN: B0018OQABU

DEDICATION

This book is dedicated to my wife TreiNise and all of my children. Thank you for your support and prayers. TreiNise, thank you for the many years together and I pray that our future years will be sweeter than our past years. To my children, thank you for allowing daddy to take time away from you in order to help people all over the world. One day this book will serve as a guide for you. Not until you are 35 though.

This book is written to help and assist singles and couples who are tired of the divorce rates and broken relationships. As you read this book, reflect on your past relationships, current relationships and if applicable, future relationships. You will laugh, cry, holler and become excited. The best enjoyment that you will find in this book is the ability to put into action what you have read.

I want to thank my editor, Tracey Vasil Biscontini for her timeless efforts and expertise in bringing this book to manifestation in the proper form. You are the best!

TABLE OF CONTENTS

KEY 1
WINNING THE HEART
& SOUL OF YOUR MATE
Page 1

KEY 2
HOW PARENTS AFFECT
YOUR RELATIONSHIPS
Page 5

KEY 3
IDEOLOGY MYTH:
MY WAY IS THE BEST WAY
Page 15

KEY 4
WHAT IS LOVE?
Page 23

KEY 5
HOW TO KEEP LOVE
IN MY RELATIONSHIP
Page 35

KEY 6
AVOIDING THE MYTHS OF MARRIAGE
Page 39

KEY 7
HAPPINESS BEGINS WITH YOU
Page 43

KEY 8
THE WORK THAT IS NEEDED
IN A RELATIONSHIP
Page 47

KEY 9
DIVORCE IS NOT AN OPTION
Page 51

KEY 10
HEALING SEXUAL FRUSTRATION
Page 55

KEY 11
THE CHEATING MATE
Page 59

KEY 12
THE CHEATING MATE PART 2
Page 63

KEY 13
DO NOT DEFRAUD ONE ANOTHER
Page 67

KEY 14
MENTAL CHEATING
Page 71

KEY 15
HIGH SEX DRIVE AND LOW SEX DRIVE
Page 75

KEY 16
FOR RICHER OR POORER
Page 77

KEY 17
MONEY ISSUES
Page 83

KEY 18
SELF COUNSELING
Page 87

KEY 19
FROM DATING TO THE "I DO" MARRIAGE
Page 91

KEY 20
COMMUNICATION DISTORTION
Page 95

KEY 21
COMMUNICATION DISTORTION PART 2
Page 99

KEY 22
COMMUNICATION DISTORTION PART 3
Page 101

SUMMATION
Page 103

INTRODUCTION

Understanding your mate is the key to a long-lasting happy relationship. People have many different theories as to why so many of us have problems with relationships. Some people believe many relationships are dysfunctional because men are from Mars and women are from Venus. Others believe that we have poor communication in relationships because men communicate internally and women communicate verbally. In my ten years of experience, I have found none of these theories to be true.

They lead us on the right path, though. The truth is men are not from Mars, and women are not from Venus. The truth is that not all men communicate internally and not all women communicate verbally. In fact, some *women* communicate internally and some men communicate *verbally*. **The truth is men and women are different because people are different.** No two people alike, be they two men or two women. If you are going to have a successful relationship, then you must understand your mate. You must understand your mate individually, not collectively. You must understand *your* mate. Some people believe that there are so many divorces in America because people don't know their mates. This premise is void, however, because many divorce cases involve couples who have been married for twenty to thirty years. These couples know each other, and have known each other, for a long time. The problem is that they have never understood each other. They know the person, but they do not know why the person is who they are.

KEY 1

WINNING THE HEART & SOUL OF YOUR MATE

When you understand your mate, you will win their heart and soul. Everyone wants to be with someone who understands them, the unique them. You need to know what makes your mate happy and why that makes them happy. During my counseling sessions, I help mates understand each other. Once they see that they have misread each other the whole duration of the relationship, a new relationship is formed. The new relationship is filled with compassion, acceptance of one's differences, and acceptance of one's weaknesses and strengths, along with patience, tolerability, charity, and love.

If you do not understand your mate, however, then you cannot fully accept your mate. If there is no accepting of your mate, then there is no love for your mate. **Love is accepting someone for who they are.** You cannot love someone for their potential. This is the relationship that says, "He/She just was not willing to change." They formulated the relationship for potential that never manifested, and therefore, the relationship was over. You cannot formulate a relationship with someone because you have known them all your life. Knowledge changes after time and experiences. You must seek to understand the person who you are with.

Love is accepting someone for who they are.

Some experts believe that money is the key to a happy relationship. Research has found that money is the number-one reason why people divorce. However, the same research states that when you view the reason for divorce, money is not as high a priority as you may think. And rich and famous people have the same relationship problems as non-rich people who are not famous. Rich people are often misunderstood because of their money and fame. Understanding your mate not only understanding who they are, but also how and why they came to be that person. Some famous people started out in an impoverished community. Once they became famous, however, their mates no longer paid attention to this impoverished community. These mates therefore have an expectation that is never met because the expectation doesn't fit who the person is and why they are who they are. If money was the key to a happy relationship, then Hollywood would not have the highest divorce among the rich. It was stated that if a marriage lasts more than two years in Hollywood, then it is a success. Understanding your mate gives you insight into the whole individual, not parts of the individual.

    Let's consider Demi Moore, for example. As a child and teen, Demi Moore did not like how she looked. Her self-esteem about her image was not good. After she became a rich star, she married Bruce Willis and had children. Then she divorced Bruce Willis and began dating a much younger man. Why did she do this? I guarantee you Bruce Willis loves Demi Moore but has never understood her. When you consider how she has changed her appearance, doesn't it make sense that she would date someone younger? She goes to great lengths to make sure she continues to look young and beautiful. She knows what it is like not to view yourself as attractive, and she never wants to go back there again. When you understand, judging ends and compassion begins.

KEY 2

HOW PARENTS AFFECT YOUR RELATIONSHIPS

Everyone begins life through the teaching of a man/woman. No child raises him- or herself. Children are raised in a certain community with its own values and traditions. They are taught in a certain place/home where they learn how to live according to the teachers in that place/house. All children have the genes of their biological mother and father. This is the reason children love their mothers and fathers no matter what. A mother or father can use crack in front of their children, and if someone talked about the parents, the child would want to fight and might have evil thoughts toward that person.

The relationship between a mother and father is significant to the relationship between a husband and a wife. The relationship between a daughter and her father is relevant to the relationship between that daughter and her husband. If the daughter likes her father, then she will get along with and like her husband. If that daughter does not like her father, however, then she will marry a man whom she loves, but does not like.

The daughter is created by the genes of her parents. If she gets along with her mother, then she will have girlfriends. If she does not get along with her mother, however, then she will not have many female friends. This principle is true because we are products of our environments. This daughter would have to formulate a relationship with her mother if she desires female friends. If her mother is deceased or is unwilling to formulate a relationship, then the daughter has to forgive her mother and learn to trust other females.

> Everyone begins life through the teaching of a man/woman.

The relationship between a man and his mother is significant to the relationship between that man and his wife. If he does not like his mother, then he will marry a woman whom he loves, but does not like. However, if he likes his mother, then he will marry a woman he gets along with. Again, this principle is true because this man has his mother's gene. Therefore, he will be automatically attracted to the gene of the mother that he carries. Now, if he wants his marriage to work with a wife whom he loves but does not like, he has to establish a relationship with his mother. If she is deceased or is unwilling to establish a relationship, then he must forgive his mother and realize that his wife is not his mother.

The relationship between a mother and father is significant to the relationship between a husband and a wife.

The relationship between a man and his father will determine if that man is going to have a lot of male friends. If a man does not know his father or has no relationship with his father, then he will not have true friendships with other men. It will be vital for that man to forgive and formulate a relationship with his father in order to establish relationships with other men.

From my experience counseling, I have learned that an ideology is the reason most people do not have good relationships with their parents. The ideology states that because you are my mother you should "xyz," and because you are my father you should "xyz." The problem with this ideology is that it does not take into account the humanness of the parents. Mothers are women who happened to have a child or children. Fathers are men who happened to have a child or children. Just because you have children does not discount your manhood or womanhood. To a child, however, parents are not regarded as human beings. but as entities.

> The relationship between a man and his father will determine if that man is going to have a lot of male friends.

This same notion can be found in marriages. When single people get married, they say, "I want a person who is like *this* and *that*," or "I want a person from God, the one who God has for me." This mindset creates several problems: (1) whenever they list the qualities they want in an individual, they fail to list the individual's imperfections. This is why so many people who date more than one person say, "If I could have *this* from this person and *that* from this other person, I would have the perfect mate." We can all conclude that there is no perfect mate. When the imperfections are revealed, however, we have a major problem within the relationship—we have *issues*.

Whenever we forget that our parents are hu-

HOW PARENTS AFFECT RELATIONSHIPS

man, we also forget that our mates are human. People are not machines or entities; they are humans who have experienced pain, hurt, love, happiness, weakness, and failure. Have you ever heard someone say, "It's not personal, it's business?" This nullifies the humanness of people. It views people as things and not humans.

Parents are the ones who develop their children's mindset. Their outlook on marriage is going to depend widely on how they were raised by their parents. Therefore, when you decide to marry or if you are married, revisit the relationship between you and your parents. It will help you understand the groundwork of your mindset about your relationship.

Wives, if you do not like your father, you may not like your husband. You will blame it on other things, but remember that your husband is not your father. If you formulate a relationship of forgiveness and humanness with your father, then you will begin to formulate a relationship of forgiveness and humanness with your husband. Husbands, it is vital for you to remember that your wife is not your mother. She may share similar qualities, but she is not your mother. Your wife may act like your mother, but she is not your mother. Seriously consider the relationship between you (husband) and your mother, and then formulate a relationship with your wife based on forgiveness and humanness.

This brings me to the second part of the relationship between mother and father: when you get married, you also marry the in-laws. I know that this may cause friction between many, but remember that the person you marry is carrying the genes of his or her parents. No matter how much you dislike your spouse's parents, if you love the person, then you at least love some parts of the parents. I know that many of you have heard that the way your spouse or potential spouse treats their parents is significant to how they are going to treat you. This concept in my opinion is true for the reasons already mentioned.

Pre-Marital Questions (Singles Only)

Here are some critical questions that I want the unmarried to answer:

1. Do you know your future in-laws?
2. What is the relationship between the mother and your boy/girlfriend?
3. What are their feelings toward their mother/father?
4. If your future mate stays the same with no adjustments, are you still willing to marry him/her?
5. What is your ideal mate and marriage?
6. What imperfections are you willing to put up with?(No one is perfect.)
7. What are your imperfections?
8. How did your imperfections contribute to your last relationship? (In other words, what negative behavior did you exhibit, what would your ex say?)
9. Is the mate you are trying, hoping, wishing, praying to marry good for your flesh or your spirit?
10. Is money (success) an issue in your decision making?
11. What sacrifices are you willing to make for the improvement/happiness of the relationship?

Marital Questions (Married Couples Only)

Here are some critical questions that I want the married couples to answer. Both parties are encouraged to answer.

1. Does your marriage consist of mercy (benefits as if the spouse has done nothing wrong)?
2. Does your marriage consist of grace (undeserved favor)?
3. Do you understand the ways/thinking of your spouse?
4. Do you understand the background (parental teachings) of your spouse?
5. What community is your spouse from, and how you think that plays a role in the marriage?
6. Do you understand why your spouse handles situations, money, and stress the way he or she does?
7. Is your spouse into a certain faith? Why or why not?
8. Does your spouse like or dislike his or her parents?
9. Does your spouse like or dislike your parents?
10. If your spouse were to cheat, why would they?
11. How often do the two of you have sex?
12. Has this time lapse increased or decreased over the last year?
13. If you have been married before, what have you learned about yourself?

14. Is the love for your spouse conditional or unconditional?

15. Do you know how you handle hurt, pain, and stress?

16. Do you know how your mate handles hurt, pain, and stress?

KEY 3

IDEOLOGY MYTH: MY WAY IS THE BEST WAY

Ideology is a concept that many people have but do not know that they have. For those of you who read the Bible, recall the children of Israel building, creating, graven images to worship. They did this when Moses was on the mountain getting the Ten Commandments from God. They formed the graven images using their minds, but they created them using various materials. When Moses saw the images, however, he was mad, so mad that he broke the stones with the Ten Commandments on them.

We are all guilty of the ideology concept. When we consider getting married or even selecting whom to date, we create an image in our mind of what we want. Then, we go on a hunt seeking and searching for that image (both male and female). Sometimes we chose the individual who comes closet to fitting the image. Other times, we sit around hoping and wishing or Mr. or Ms. Right to show up. The amazing part is that the Mr. or Ms. Right is the person who fits the image that we have created in our minds.

We form this image for many reasons. Sometimes after we have been with someone, we decide that the next person we date will not be like this person. It is most interesting that we select the negative to not exist in the new person, but we often fail to remember and recall the positive. This becomes apparent and funny when the new person does not have the good qualities that the old person possessed.

Ideology is a concept that many people have but do not know that they have.

We formulate the ideology according to our parents. Some women want a man like their father, while others want a man unlike their father, and some women just want a father type (love, support, take care of, correct, lead, reject, control—you get the point). Some men want a person who is like their mother, some men want a person who is unlike their mother, and some men want a mother (caring, babysitting, taking care of, nurturing—you get the

IDEOLOGY MYTH: MY WAY IS THE BEST WAY

point). We also formulate this type of thinking according to our friends, associates, church members, church leaders, and the media.

Our friends influence what we want because we care about how we are perceived by our friends. I did not say by our enemies, but by our friends. We like it when people perceive us as respected, praised, and honored. Let's be honest; it feels *great*. Therefore, we tend to chose someone who will make us look good in front of our friends. This is the reason why appearance is important.

> **We formulate the ideology according to our parents.**

We want someone who we can brag about. This is why occupation is important. If you think that occupation is important only because of money, consider what you would do if the person loses their job. Are you in or out?

Our associates play a very important role in the mindset of the kind of person you want. This is because our associates see us on a daily basis. Can you imagine having your associates see you kissing a "bum look-a-like?" "Oh God, what would they think of me?" "Baby you got to be crazy. Meet me around the corner for a kiss." However, if that someone was attractive to the associates, *what a kiss!*

Our selection of a mate is also based on the opinions of church members and the church leader or leaders. *Oh my God!* Now let's see. Ladies, have you brought every man that you have dated to church with you? Gentlemen, uh huh, have you brought every woman that you have dated to church with you? Or, have you only gone to church with the man/woman to whom you are with now? Whatever happened to let everyone come into the church? We will witness all.

Our friends influence what we want because we care about how we are perceived by our friends.

The attitudes and judgments of the church have a huge influence on the person we chose as our mate. If the church disagrees with your selection, the man/woman who loves you, what would you do and is this just as important as how you feel? I wonder if you will still attend that church. I believe that it is important to add that if the church is going to help you select a mate, then that same church should help you with the troubles and issues that come with this selection. But, often times, the church abandons people when it appears that the relationship is over. As a pastor, I re-

IDEOLOGY MYTH: MY WAY IS THE BEST WAY

spect the decision of individuals as long as they have an understanding about the person they are selecting, but, regardless, will support the staying together of all marriages without judgment. I will not counsel couples about these two things, however: cheating and physical abuse. I will counsel people individually about these issues but not as a couple.

Our last way of formulating the ideology of a mate is through the media. The media causes us to want the lifestyle that we see, hear about, and read about. The most interesting thing about media reporters is that they never give us the whole truth. We see couples on television and think *wow*, but two years later, they are divorced. What happened? Media reporters never tell us. They often take us into a fantasy world but will not bring us out of this word and into reality. Therefore, we formulate a relationship based on fantasy rather than reality.

> **The attitudes and judgments of the church have a huge influence on the person we chose as our mate.**

Here are some critical questions:
1.   *What is your ideal mate?*
2.   *What is your ideal marriage/relationship?*

3. Where is your ideal place to live?
4. Who are your ideal neighbors?
5. What is your ideal church?
6. How did you formulate these ideals?

In my opinion, **ideologies do not work because they always leave out the mate's negatives traits or imperfections, the areas he/she needs to improve upon or develop. We never include what we are willing to put up with and endure. Ideologies only take into account the positive.** Unfortunately, this is the reason that so many people are single. Singles who wish to marry often know the type of person they desire, and they think that they will find this person without any imperfections. Without the imperfections, however, the so-called image and desired person does not exist. Learning to live with imperfections is the key to staying in a committed relationship. Single people would agree that meeting people is not the real problem. The real problem is discovering their imperfections.

I wonder what would happen to humankind

if we learned to live with each other's imperfections. Can you imagine the difference in society or in the community in which you live? Let's start in your house. Think about how many marriages have failed, were destroyed, because people could not live with their mates' imperfections. Now let's discuss how to live with imperfect people. Living with imperfect people is difficult. Sometimes the imperfections also make you appear imperfect.

> **We never include what we are willing to put up with and endure. Ideologies only take into account the positive.**

KEY 4

WHAT IS LOVE?

Love is a creative process. People who choose to love someone must understand that love is action. It is more than mere words formed after you have gotten to know someone. One of the problems with the words "I love you" is that one-time love doesn't always mean forever love. We hear how people break up because they do not have the love they once had. People can get over someone whom they once loved because the process has stopped. Whenever you stop the process of love, you are headed in the direction of getting over someone.

Love is a continual process. People who want to maintain their love must maintain the process of love. The process of love consists of having compassion for someone in the midst of every new situation.

It is amazing how often compassion stops when someone produces a situation in which compassion is needed. For example, if a mate is sick, then compassion is needed, and if the sick person's mate loves them, then the person will show compassion. However, if the same sick mate needs to be taken care of financially, physically, or patiently, a new compassion is needed. Have you ever heard these words *in action*: "I will love you so long as…?"

Another process for loving is forgiveness. Forgiveness is important because many people can forgive their mates for something, sometimes, but when you ask them to continually forgive to keep their love ongoing, they think you are asking a lot. I don't believe that you need an example of forgiveness.

> Love is a creatve process

You already know what it means to forgive. Sharing and commitment are other action terms in the processes for loving. When you consider sharing and commitment, I want you to consider consistency. Consistency is the key. Many can share sometimes, and commitment can last for a season, but consistency gets love going. If you have ever cheated on someone or have been cheated on by someone whom you never thought would cheat on you, then you understand. If someone has called you selfish before, or if you have called someone selfish, then the question is, "Do they share sometimes?" If the answer is yes, then there is love, but no consistency; therefore the love is possibly temporal.

Love is not only a process, it is a creative process. **Love is creative because your love for one person is different from your love for someone else.** You cannot love everyone the same. If have been divorced and are married or even if you have an ex somewhere, you do not love the new person like you loved your ex. Many people misunderstand this process. This is one of the reasons why people tend to love so quickly and easily. People who love quickly and easily do not understand that love is creative. They tend to love everyone the same.

> Love is a continual process

Love is give and take. Give and take is not dealing with issues at this point. Love is give and take means that one has to give love and one has to take love. When you begin to understand your mate, you will see that people find it difficult to love their mates and that people find it difficult to receive love from their mates. This is why someone is always working harder to keep the relationship together than someone else.

No one wants to be in a relationship where they give love but never receive it.

This notion of giving love but never receiving love creates a problem because if you were to ask the two mates, they would disagree with each other. Often the definition of love is different. If I define love as sharing and you do not have anything to share, then I would conclude that you do not love me. However, if you define love as being taken care of, then you would say that you do love me and that I love you, especially if you are taking care of the house from a domestic perspective.

> Another process for loving is forgiveness

The difficulty with receiving love is where one of the mates finds themselves. Many people who find it difficult to love tend to push away those who want them and go after those who don't. I have counseled many people who loved those who hurt them and did not make them feel confident about themselves. Have you ever heard someone say, "I don't want to mess up the friendship?" Such people are not used to people treating them with respect. Some people are more interested in the rough side of individuals, both male and female.

It is important to understand why people are

this way. Some people grew up in an environment where love meant abuse. If there was no abuse, then there was no love or no relationship. This section is not intended to judge anyone, but rather to give an understanding as to why people are the way that they are. Consider an environment where the father abused the mother and the mother enjoyed it (at least in front of the children). A normal day for this family is one in which Father verbally abused Mother during the day and laughed with her at night. The children may or may not like the day relationship between Father and Mother, but the night relationship is the best. When the children decide whom to date, giving or receiving abuse will be in the picture. Consider another situation: a woman is told by every guy in the neighborhood that she is unattractive or weighs too much. When she attends high school and college, she hears the same thing. At home with her parents, she is told that she is too fat and this is why no one wants her. She finally graduates from college, receives a great-paying job and goes out on her first date, which was set up by

> **Love is creative because your love for one person is different from your love for someone else.**

her friend. Lo and behold the man likes her. He tells her that she is attractive and smart. Can you foresee what is going on in her mind? "He's lying. What does he want? He is just like the others." She might also be thinking, "I am going to marry him now before he changes his mind." If the first is true, then we understand how and why she is thinking that way.

This notion of giving love but never receiving love creates a problem because if you were to ask the two mates, they would disagree with each other.

Let's assume the later is true, and she wants to marry him right away. She discovers, however, that he only wanted her money and that he would not marry her if his life depended on it. Can you foresee her next date? Can you see this woman as part of a couple? Many of you would conclude that she has low self-esteem. I would disagree. Her self-esteem is not low when it comes to education and work-related issues. When it comes to relationships, however, she needs someone who will understand her. Stating that a person has low self-esteem is a judgment. This woman is struggling with receiving love, because she has never received it before. If someone would take the time to understand her, she would struggle at first, but would later be one of the happiest women in the world because she knows that she is deserving of love. Remember the whole framework of this book is understanding your mate.

While some mates find it difficult to receive love, others find it difficult to give love. They usually make remarks like, "There is nothing wrong with taking care of me. Is there?" Many people call them selfish, when really some people do not know how to love someone outside of their family or themselves. For example, consider a man who was raised as an only child. He never had to share with anyone is his home except for his parents. His parents always gave to him, but he never had to give back in order for this to happen. He gets into a relationship and now he is having trouble. Can you see why? His mate may not understand why he appears selfish. He finds it difficult to love because maybe he never had to love. Can you imagine how he defines love? Let us imagine ourselves as this person. I want you to take a minute and define love. I can guarantee you that your mate will not define love the way you

> **The difficulty with receiving love is where one of the mates finds themselves.**

would if you were this person.

Also, you will find that the way you define love is the way that you love. This is why understanding your mate has not been a part of the relationship equation. People only treat people the way that they want to be treated. When you treat people how you want to be treated, you treat them with care, compassion, and honesty—moral terms that make your community worth living in. There are other reasons why people find it difficult to give love. I do not want to give you the other reasons because the reasons I can give may not fit your mate. You have to seek to understand your mate and why your mate is the way that they are. Every mate is different and needs to be treated differently. The more you understand your mate, the less likely you are to judge and misinterpret your mate's actions. If you feel that your mate is selfish, ask yourself why you think they are this way. You probably know *how* your mate acts selfishly, but I want you to find to *why* they are selfish.

While some mates find it difficult to receive love, others find it difficult to give love.

There are many singles today who find it difficult to love again. Many say, "It seems like everybody who said they loved me only gave me pain." Let's try to understand people who find it difficult to love again. We know that love has meant pain for them. Therefore, we know that they have been hurt before. Do you think that they were hurt in a marriage or couple relationship? We also know that they were disappointed. They may have been with someone whom they thought would never hurt them. It is also possible that they received what they believed to be verbal abuse. I say *believed to be verbal abuse* because maybe they cannot tell the difference between verbal abuse and constructive criticism. Can you imagine the next relationship that this person is in? The new mate is giving them hard-nose information about their circumstance and they feel attacked. If the new mate does not understand this person, the relationship will be over before it gets started.

There are many singles today who find it difficult to love again.

Many people who find it hard to love again may date again or even marry, but they are not going to put their whole heart into it. They tend to make a rational decision about the relationship and whom to date as opposed to an emotional decision. You have heard people say, "Let's live together first."

People say things like this when they do not want to get hurt again. They want to make sure, rationally, that the relationship is going to work. Some may live with someone, but never marry because of the fear of getting hurt. Nevertheless, there is no way to love again without taking the risk of getting hurt again.

> **Many people who find it hard to love again may date again or even marry, but they are not going to put their whole heart into it.**

Some experts have reported that compatibility is the key to a lasting happy relationship. I disagree because compatibility is knowing that you and another person agree with certain behaviors. Knowledge changes as the relationship changes. People can be compatible today and not compatible five years from now. Should people only date until the compatibility runs out? The key to having a lasting, happy relationship is understanding your mate. If you seek to understand the one you are with, then you will be understood. Understanding your mate is a constant thought process. It stops you from judging and allows you to accept differences. When you understand your mate, you are forced to feel compassion for them.

People who find it difficult to love again have not learned that love has a different meaning for different people. The toughest question to ask is, "What do you mean when you say 'I love you?'" Once a person who finds it difficult to love again can answer this question and ask this question from an understanding point of view, they will be willing to risk getting hurt again. The danger in getting hurt from a relationship is when you do not know why you got hurt, or more importantly, why the person hurt you. Understanding your mate will give you the answers. Look back at your previous relationships, seek to understand your mate, and you will discover why the relationship ended the way that it did, and why your previous mate made certain decisions and performed certain actions.

KEY 5

HOW TO KEEP LOVE IN MY RELATIONSHIP

Every relationship must have a loving environment. The key is to create a loving environment. To begin, let's consider your current or past environment: is/was everyone free to be themselves in the environment and be happy? This is an interesting concept because you cannot find the whole answer without involving your mate. You may have been free to be yourself, but that does not mean your mate is/was free to be him- or herself and be happy. It is one thing to be free to be yourself. It is another to be free to be yourself *and* be happy. Free to be yourself is when you are doing (dressing, shopping, looking, working, etc.) and saying (expressing) what you want based on how you are or the way you operate. However, free to be yourself and be happy consists of not hearing any anti-you slurs or behaviors from your mate. Many people are receiving rebuttals whenever they do or say something that is different from their mate.

If a relationship does not have a loving environment, then the people within the relationship will be one way in the environment and another way outside of the environment. I always hear that people in relationships want to be friends and even best friends. Remember, friends are developed because people are free to be themselves with someone without being judged or rebuked. When you see you mate enjoying themselves better with someone else, I want you to ask yourself a critical question: "Is my mate free to be themselves and be happy around me?" If your answer is no, then you have a problem. The problem is that you do not understand your mate. You are judging their differences. You wish that they were more like you, and because they are not like you, they are not free to be themselves and be happy.

Every relationship must have a loving environment.

Many relationships have ended because people were not free to be themselves and be happy around their mate. You can only imagine the number of men and women who have cheated on their mates because they found it easier to be happy with someone else.

Here is a famous line: "I love you but I am not in love with you." Some of you have heard it and have said it. When a person says that they love you but they are not in love with you, what they are saying is that they are not free to be themselves around you. You make them feel unworthy, sad, stupid, and no good as a person. Can any relationship last when a person feels like this? Creating a loving environment is the answer to a happy home. A loving environment exists when people are seeking to understand one another. When you understand your mate, you will accept their differences. Their differences will not cause you to feel out of order. Accepting your mate's differences will enhance your relationship. You will discover that you need to incorporate some of those differences in your life. For example, maybe your mate always wants the house to be super clean. You do not mind the house being clean but you do not think it needs to be super clean. If you understand your mate and know why they want the house to be immaculate, then you will value the cleanliness.

KEY 6

AVOIDING THE MYTHS OF MARRIAGE

There are many myths about marriage. **In this section, I want to tell you these myths and how they developed and teach you how to avoid believing these myths.** This section is what I call marriage ideology. Marriage ideology is simply what you think a marriage is and should be. It is your thinking of what marriage is and what it should be that creates the myth. Your thinking is a myth because in the midst of your thinking, you never consider the other person. For example, people say, "My marriage is going to be filled with love and my mate is going to treat me like a queen/king." What if your mate knows nothing about the treatment of queens/kings? This is the myth. You get married, and when your mate doesn't treat you the way you want to be treated, the marriage is over. You never take the time to understand your mate, nor does your mate take the time to understand why you want to treated like a queen/king. And no, not everyone wants to be treated like this. Remember, everyone is different and you are different from everyone. When marriages last for a short time, less than five years, it is because a myth was formulated prior to the marriage, and when the reality doesn't fit the myth, the relationship ends.

A wife who I was counseling stated that her husband should do everything and anything to make her happy. My question to her was, "Whose marriage is this?" She was making the same mistake as many others. She was living in her myths about the marriage. She is living according to the myth that says, "You are my mate and you should…" Ladies and gentlemen, this is a myth. People are different because they have unique backgrounds and experiences. **As you are considering your relationship or past/potential relationship, answer this question: "Whose relationship is it?"** I hope that when you answer this question, you look at the behaviors, and not your own point of view. Many people fall into the myth because they believe that their life is the best life for the relationship. After all, their parents

There are many myths about marriage.

were married and lasted. Therefore, they know what is best and what the relationship should be like. If they did not like their parents' relationship, then they structure the relationship to be unlike their parents' relationship. The problem is that their relationship/marriage does not belong to only them—it belongs to them and to their mate.

I have to give credit to the myth, because the myth is great for those who wish to remain single. **Have you heard someone say, "I rather be by myself. I can do bad all by myself." My question is, "Why would you want to do bad all by yourself?" There is no help when you are doing bad all by yourself.** The key is to adjust your thinking so that you understand your mate. Most people who live under this myth want to be understood. In order to be understood, however, they must first understand. Understanding your mate takes away the pressure of wanting things your way and allows you to embrace someone else. When you embrace someone else, you add value to yourself. This phenomenon occurs in every facet of life. When you understand a different culture's way of living, you add value to your life. When you understand your colleague's way of selling or solving problems, you add value to yourself. You will also gain an understanding as to why you are different and why you handle matters the way that you do. You will understand yourself.

> **"Whose relatonship is it?"**

KEY 7

HAPPINESS BEGINS WITH YOU

There is a concept in the marriage ideology that one mate tends to unconsciously imitate the other: *I want to worship you.* One of the mates tends to want someone to worship them. They say things like, "If you loved me you would…" *"I am not happy because you…"* and *"I've always wanted a mate who has…, therefore you need to get…"* These are all myths that people have about marriage. These myths move individuals to try and be understood, but the goal is to understand. When you are seeking to be understood, you will find yourself frustrated and discouraged. The comment that people will never change therefore the relationship is over is a classic. Someone is trying to be understood in order to be worshiped. However, such a relationship will be filled with anger and pain.

"If you loved me you would. . ." has created pain in the lives of many. Relationships are unions between two lives/lifestyles. In other words, before the relationship started, people were living life their way. Now that a relationship has formed, the necessary adjustments have not taken place. Sometimes someone within the relationship does not want to give up their lifestyle. Whatever they want to happen within the relationship is normally the best thing or the most comfortable behavior—for the individual, however, and not for both parties. This is why I ask the question, "Whose marriage/relationship is it?" because one person wants the other to come into their world, but they are not willing to come into the other person's world. For example, another wife who I counseled was angry with her husband because he wants to spend time with his family and friends. She feels that he is married and should spend time with her and do away with exces-

> "I am not happy because you..." and "I've always wanted a mate who has..., therefore you need to get..."

sive time with his family and friends. Some of you may agree, but he is a divorced male who in the past found comfort in family and friends. Spending time with his siblings and friends became his refuge. Now that he is married, do you really think that he is going to change his lifestyle? His wife is an only child. She has no siblings to spend time with. Her friends are too few and she wants to be in the house with her husband. As a resolution, it is critical for the wife to understand the husband for who and how he is, and it is essential for the husband to understand his wife and why she feels the way that she does. Can you as a reader see why understanding your mate is the answer to many issues couples face? I always tell everyone, "You must be willing to understand your mate. You have to want to understand them."

> **"If you loved me you would..." has created pain in the lives of many.**

KEY 8

THE WORK THAT IS NEEDED IN A RELATIONSHIP

Understanding your mate takes effort. You have to come out of what you think is right or best and understand how and why your mate functions that way they do. Do you remember when you were in grade school and the teacher wanted you to do an assignment and you did not understand why? Your effort was small. Compare that to when you got an assignment and you understood why it was important. During my freshmen year in college, I found it hard to know which notes were important and which were not. Therefore, I tried to take notes on everything. Later, I learned the key terminologies that the professor would use when the information was important. The point is that I needed the professor to provide the information for me, what I thought about what was going to be on the test was wrong. Your way of thinking when it comes to your mate is likely wrong if you don't understand your mate. You have to forget about what you think is right and understand your mate to see how they think and why they think this way.

When mates find it difficult to decide that they are going to understand each other, they are usually tired, frustrated, and unwilling to give any more effort. I ask mates, "How long did you plan to be married?" The obvious answer is forever, but then I say, "If your mate has been responding to situations their normal way for two years, why is the relationship over when you have at least fifty more years to go before you reach the forever point?" Marriages, unlike dating relationships, are a sentence for life. The classic example I give is about a man who has been sentenced to spend his natural life in prison. Natural life means that he is never getting out. He tells his friends and family that he is getting out because his attorney was working with the prosecuting attorney. He states that he is innocent and is filing for an appeal. When he gets into the prison where he will be for the rest

Understanding your mate takes effort.

THE WORK THAT IS NEEDED IN A RELATIONSHIP

of his life, he has a hard time. He does not adjust to his new situation and therefore struggles. He finds himself in trouble with the officers and in fights with the other inmates. However, after he comes into the reality that he is not getting out and prison is where he will be for the rest of his life, he makes the best out of it. It is at this point that he spends time learning about prison life. He begins to educate himself in order to better himself. He becomes so well-versed that he is now welcoming the new inmates into the system. This man now respects prison and sees it as a home and not his enemy.

> As long as divorce is an option, you will not dedicate yourself to it.

In order for any relationship to work, the parties involved must be in it to stay. *As long as divorce is an option, you will not dedicate yourself to it.*

KEY 9
DIVORCE IS NOT AN OPTION

DIVORCE CANNOT BE AN OPTION. The door of the possibly of divorce must become a wall. As long as the door of divorce is open, you will not submit your entire heart, soul, and mind into the relationship. You will always hold some of *you* back. It is amazing to me how some relationships consist of one person who wants a divorce and another person who does not want a divorce. The person who does not want the divorce is living the marriage like their life. In order words, people have not made the adjustment to their situation. Like the man in prison, once he decided that he is not leaving, the adjustment started. Once you decide that you are not leaving the marriage no matter what, the adjustments will be made. I can also conclude that the mate who wants a divorce does not understand the other mate. The critical question is whether they want to understand this person. More often than not, they have run out of their resources on how to *change* their mate's behavior. Once they are introduced to the key resource in understanding your mate, the relationship will take on a new romance. When you understand your mate, romance is an everyday enjoyment.

Before a person considers divorce, they usually spend a lot of time thinking about how they can get out of the relationship. If you count how many times you have thought about how you can get out of your relationship, you will be amazed. You will be even more amazed at how many times your mate is trying to figure out how they can get out of the relationship. The reason that they are asking this question is because they believe that the situation is going to last forever. The moment that a person believes that their negative situation is going to last forever, the thought of divorce or breakup occurs. Situations in relationships do not last forever. Nonetheless, if you begin to understand your mate, then you get an understanding of how the situations came about. One of the most frustrating mindsets in a relationship is not understanding why the relationship is going through difficult times. If you blame your mate for the relationship having difficulties, then you do not understand your mate. If you solely blame yourself, then you are with someone who does not understand you. Understanding your mate gives you access to the reasons why decisions occur the way that they do. Once you have an understanding of your relationship through understanding your mate, then you gain power to change the circumstance. Circumstances change when people are working toward change with the right mindset. If your mindset is "I have to change my mate," then you are not understanding your mate. If your mindset is "I have to take a look in the mirror," then you are on the path but not in the door/house. The focus has to be on understanding your mate.

KEY 10

HEALING SEXUAL FRUSTRATION

Now we come to the part of the book that many have been anticipating: healing sexual frustration. What do you do when you are sexually frustrated with your mate? **First of all, it is important to understand that sex is a must.** The reason why sex is a must is because it gives you the relaxation to handle the issues that occur in relationships. **Sex does not cure problems. It only gives you the relaxation to handle the problems.** Sex is so important that before divorce comes, there is a lack of sex. If you are divorced, how long before the divorce did you go without sex? I will tell you that if you keep the sex alive and active, divorce will be pushed back. It is critical for me to add that sex is better when you understand your mate. Knowing your mate helps in this area, but it limits you after your mate becomes used to you while understanding your mate moves you into other areas that are pleasing to your mate. Has your mate become bored with your sex? Have they told you? If the answer to these questions is yes, then you do not understand your mate. Understanding your mate moves sexual boredom into sexual experimentation. I think I need to say that again: **understanding your mate moves sexual boredom into sexual experimentation.** Understanding your mate will give you the strength and confidence to come out of your comfort zone. The comfort zone of sexual activity creates boredom. When sex is boring, all kinds of complaints begin. Did you know that it is hard to argue when sex is awesome? The clothing on the floor, bills not paid on time, and kids acting up is not worth breaking up over. Sex gives you the relaxation to handle these issues. Now I can hear many of you saying that sex does not pay the bills. If you are saying that, then your mate needs to understand you, because you are getting *awesome* sex. **When your mate is complaining**

When your mate is complaining about everything, and you cannot do any thing to please them, try providing awesome sex.

about everything, and you cannot do any thing to please them, try providing awesome sex. Trust me when I tell you, your mate is asking for some great sex. They are begging and pleading for it. Provide it to your mate and I guarantee you that the complaining will stop. This method is true for both men and women.

KEY 11
THE CHEATING MATE

When I discuss sexual frustration, I must include understanding the cheating mate. The critical question asked among people is, *"Where is the black book?"* Sometimes the cheater is asking the question, and sometimes the one who is being cheated on is asking the question. There are three philosophical reasons why people cheat and three critical reasons. I am not going to give you my philosophical reasons because if you do not agree with my philosophy then you will devalue the information. So for my *three critical reasons* as to why people cheat: **everyone wants to be in a loving environment.** If your mate is in an environment where they are not free to be themselves and be happy, then they are more likely to search for an environment where they can be themselves and be happy. They will find themselves flirting more, when I say more I mean switching numbers, talking to the opposite sex late at night about non-business matters (trying to get turned on). **Everyone wants to be themselves and be happy.** Some people have been hurt so much that they now refuse to be unhappy. They will cheat and think it is okay and justifiable. When you understand your mate, you will create the environment where they are free to be themselves and be happy. Another client of mine believes that her husband is cheating on her. Without making speculations, I listened to her. Truthfully, I do not know if he is cheating or not. I am totally against cheating, but the point of this section is to give understanding. I asked her several questions about her mate.

Everyone wants to be themselves and be happy.

Through the questions, I discovered that her mate is an orderly person who loves to dress in uniform. He enjoys things to be in order and he operates his life this way. He is a very structured person, one that you might conclude has made a career in the armed forces. When he comes home, his wife only wants to discuss issues within their marriage. She is a stay-at-home mom of three children. She believes that he is cheating. I want you to remember that the reason she is discussing this issue is because she feels hurt. The home is not clean and has no structure and the children have a ball all over the place. Based on this information from an understanding perspective, is this husband at home a lot? If you answered no, you are correct. The environment sends him away. He cannot handle an environment that is not structured and clean. I asked his wife, "If he is cheating, what kind of environment do you think the woman he is cheating with is presenting to him?"

> **Everyone wants to be in a loving environment.**

KEY 12

THE CHEATING MATE
PART 2

You see, I need you to understand my style of counseling. I do not take sides. I give people an understanding of their situation and their mates. After they demonstrate that they understand their situation and mate, then I give them an understanding of themselves. I told this wife to become the best wife that she can be, to become the best domestic engineer that she can be, and to understand her mate and watch the change in his behavior. Now when her husband comes home and sees the house is clean and structured and his children are behaving, he wants to stay there with the family. Some of you may be wondering why I talked to the wife about changing her ways and not the husband. It is because she was the one who came to me. If the husband had come to me, then I would have talked to him about changing his ways. The responsibility is on the one who has the information. You have to be the best mate that you can be. Trying to find people who will agree with you does not give you the resources you need. What people need the most is understanding; then they will discover their own resources for help. The resources are different depending on you and your mate.

People do not want their negatives thrown in their face. Whenever a mate feels like their negatives are always thrown in their face, they will rebel. People tend to lose self-esteem and self-worth when they only hear negative things about themselves. Some people use sex as a refuge to feel better about themselves. They will have sex with someone they just met or with an ex. Their goal is to have sex with someone who makes them feel like a good person. You will also notice that when a person has their negatives and/or issues thrown in their face, their sexual desire goes down. If you want to turn your mate off, start talking to them about their weaknesses, negative behaviors, and/or past failures. You will send them to another room.

The third reason why people cheat is because ***relationships are too much responsibility.*** People tend to run from the responsibility of relationships. When you are having sex with multiple partners, there is no responsibility to one person. Let's face it, the real you is revealed when you are with one person. But if you have multiple partners, no one knows who you are. Some have concluded that relationships are too much work. It is true that sometimes people do not want to change.

Effective relationships will cause people to change. The good news is that effective relationships will change for the better. Many people believe that happiness comes from within. This belief occurs when someone feels that their mate is not making them happy. As a comeback, the mate replies, "It is not my responsibility to make you happy. Happiness comes from within." The truth of the matter is that happiness only comes from within when it has been put within the mate. No one starts off happy. Happiness must be given first, and then one can refer to the happiness that they have inside.

Therefore, ***it is the responsibility of a mate to make or give the other person happiness.*** Now, if you do not have happiness, then I understand that you cannot give happiness. You cannot give what you don't have. Whenever you hear of someone saying, "It is not my job to make you happy," what they are saying is, **"The responsibility is not mine to make you happy."** How can the responsibility not be the mate's? If this is true, then how does the relationship gain happiness? Have you ever heard someone say, "My mate makes me so happy?"

> **Effective relationships will cause people to change.**

KEY 13

DO NOT DEFRAUD ONE ANOTHER

If the relationship is going to receive sexual healing, then people must not hold back. Although it is more important to understand why someone is holding back opposed to just wanting them to give it up, sometimes people are holding back because they are mad and do not want to be touched. People use their emotions to decide whether they are going to sexually involve themselves with their mate. The truth is sexual involvement may change how you are feeling about being mad. Some people threaten their mates: **"If you don't do what I say and/or what I want, I am not going to give you any sex."** Sex becomes a vehicle to get people to do what you want them to do. It becomes a power tool for the person who is being asked for sex.

If the woman is asking the man, then he has the power. If the man is asking the woman for sex, then she has the power. It is not to be used as a power play to get people to do what you want them to do. Sex is to be enjoyed by each other. Sometimes, the person may want sex a certain kind of way, for example oral sex, and the mate is not willing to provide oral sex. The person who wants oral sex becomes frustrated and does not want the sex at all. Is this fair? Is this right? The critical question is does the mate who wants sex understand why the mate wants oral sex? If the mate understands the reason the mate wants oral sex, then a compromising decision can be made. Maybe oral sex is asked for as proof that love is in the relationship. Maybe oral sex is used as a way to have power over the mate. Maybe oral sex is wanted because without it, the sex is not enjoyable for both parties. Whatever the reason, gaining an understanding helps sex to take place in the marriage.

If the relationship is going to receive sexual healing, then people must not hold back.

Have you ever heard or spoken the sentence, "All you want is my sex/body." A mate who says this does not feel loved or valued unless sex is present.

DO NOT DEFRAUD ONE ANOTHER

When sex is not present, they feel zero existence from the mate. They want conversation and social activity outside of sex. When you have this understanding, you can provide the care and comfort that your mate needs so that they will enjoy sex with you. As long as your mate feels that you do not want them outside of sex, they will not enjoy having sex with you. I believe that they will hold back so that you cannot enjoy it as much, either. Their mind is saying, "Why should you have all the fun?" This creates what I call mental cheating.

KEY 14
MENTAL CHEATING

Mental cheating is when you are in bed with your mate, but your mind is with someone else. Have you heard the song by the Ojays, "Your body here with me, but your mind is on the other side of town?" I guess I could ask you if you have ever mentally cheated on your mate. Do not answer; it is not a question. Why would someone in the video take their mind to the other side of town, down the street, or next door? They do this because they are not turned on by their mate. They are searching for someone who can turn them on. They are searching for an arousal. You want to ask yourself why you are not giving your mate the arousal necessary for sexual pleasure.

I must add this note: sometimes your mate is

calling your name during the activity, but are thinking about someone else. What did you do to them before the sexual activity started? Were they upset with you for any reason? If you are experiencing this with your mate, seek to understand why, and then you will have the necessary answers to turn their focus back on you. Also stop messing with their mind. You cannot play games with them first, and then be ready for the real thing. When people are in the mood for sex, they are ready. Depending on your mate, the playing may cause them to feel that you do not really want to have sex with them. Understanding your mate will allow you to know what games to play and how long to play them. You will also learn how to reinforce your mate to know that sex is going to take place.

Mental cheating is when you are in bed with your mate, but your mind is with someone else.

In order for people to enjoy sex, proper blood flow must be present. If you do not have proper blood flow, then enjoyment to the satisfaction will not occur. This is why people have complained about not having organisms. They are not receiving proper blood flow. Their mind is not focused on the task at hand; therefore blood is blocked somewhere. People with diabetes suffer from blood flow problems and often need medication to help their blood circulate properly. Understanding this information is important because people often see themselves as being unable when the issue can be due to health problems. High blood pressure, stress, and a feeling of low self-esteem can also contribute to a blockage in blood flow. Understanding your mate is the key to opening a life filled with sexual happiness.

KEY 15

HIGH SEX DRIVE & LOW SEX DRIVE

The last point I want to explain regarding healing sexual frustration is that *some mates have a high sex drive and some have a low sex drive.* The more you understand about your mate's sex drive, the more you are able to enjoy sex with them. Consider a person who has a low sex drive married to a person with a high sex drive. Right away, we can conclude that sexually there will be some challenges. If the two have great understanding when communicating, then sexually they will be pleased. If there is misunderstanding, however, frustration will be the least of their problems. The high-sex-drive mate will say that their mate never wants to have sex with them.

The high-sex-drive mate may believe that their mate is cheating. They may believe that they are not good enough. They may believe that they are missing what their mate wants. Without understanding, many speculations take place. People start making decisions and taking actions based on speculations. The worst case is that someone leaves a relationship based on speculation and later learns that the speculation was not true. Do not speculate; understand your mate. People have low and high sex drives for many reasons. Understanding your mate's sex drive and why it exists is the breakthrough to a happy sex life.

> **Some mates have a high sex drive and some have a low sex drive.**

KEY 16
FOR RICHER OR POORER

The statistics state that money is believed to be the number-one reason why people divorce. The statistics also state that people who have divorced over money is a low percentage. These statistics lead me to discuss the phrase *"**for richer or poorer.**"* It is funny that many couples who are marrying do not want this phrase as part of their wedding vows because it does not say *how* poor. Is there anyone reading this who wants a mate who is broke? How broke can your mate be before you think the marriage is in trouble? One young woman stated, "When his brokenness messes with my credit, the relationship is over." What about you? Do you understand why someone is where they are financially? Understanding your mate can give you the reason and thus help the person to move to a better place financially.

Understanding your mate can allow your mate to assist in other areas as opposed to bringing home money. Do you see how understanding is the key? Sometimes the mate with the most money asks the question, "Do you want me or the money?" Singles with money often struggle with this question. It's a critical question to answer because sometimes the person wants someone to want them. They forget that the money is part of them, at least at this point. They want the money to be separate from them but it is not. Movie stars have this problem as well; they will not date someone who does not have the kind of money they have. Why? They believe that a person with less money will want their money and not them.

> The statistics state that money is believed to be the number-one reason why people divorce

This book is not written to pick sides, but rather to give an understanding. Everyone wants someone who wants them for them, but when there is more about you externally, like a lot of money, big body parts (breasts, booty, etc.), or an expensive car, people who do not have the same type of possessions will take longer to want the individual. Halle Berry faces this challenge. Most people regard her as being so attractive that it will take them a longer time to understand her as a person. Her attractiveness makes people ignore who she is. I wonder if Halle Berry views herself as being attractive. Some people do not see themselves as being attractive; they see what they feel. Let me say that again: **They do not see themselves as being attractive but see what they feel.**

They do not see themselves as being attractive but see what they feel. The person who does not have as much money believes that if they had money, they would be treated differently. They believe that money is being used as power over them. Why do they feel this way? Do they understand what goes on in the mind of someone who has money but is with someone who does not? Understanding your mate is critical to any relationship. When you do not understand your mate, you will have insufficient evidence for your feelings. It is possible that your mate is not using their money over you; they just want some appreciation for paying the bills and for vacation, groceries, clothing, etc. The truth be told, life is better with money.

Relationships are better with money, but if you do not have an understanding you still end up frustrated, hurt, and as in many cases, divorced. Understanding your mate can also give you the information as to why your mate wants to lead a more conservative life. Maybe they do not want to end up broke. Maybe they do not want to be like others they know. Maybe they want an image. Maybe their image is important to them and money helps this image. Do not think that I am referring to women. Remember, not all women are the same and not all men are the same. I know a man who gets his haircut three times a week, and I know a woman who gets her hair done twice a week. This suggests that some men care more about their looks than some women do.

Some people who are struggling do not want to be seen as struggling. So they live a lifestyle that portrays a successful person when the truth is that they are struggling financially. When people know you are struggling, they can be judgmental. Therefore, one may feel that it is better to pretend and not be judged then to live out the truth and be judged. When you understand a person who functions like this, you can acquire the tools to help this person. The truth is people are going to judge you no matter what. People judge the rich and the poor. The key is in understanding your mate. When you understand your mate, you will not judge their spending habits, but rather negotiate in order to create happiness within the relationship. When you understand your mate, you will also continue to try to improve your mate's circumstances. Your mate will view you as their personal counselor when you understand them.

> **Some people who are struggling do not want to be seen as struggling.**

KEY 17
MONEY ISSUES

Many relationships have money issues because someone has decided that they are going to spend money on certain things no matter what. Have you ever heard someone say, *"I am going to get my hair done and I don't care what you say"*? This person has made up their mind that it is critically important for them to get and keep their hair done. Remember this person can be a man or a woman. Understanding your mate will give you the ability to discover why it is important for them to get their hair done. Perhaps their outer image is important to them because when they were younger they were teased and talked about negatively. As they have gotten older, they do not want to experience the negativity anymore. Spending money on their hair helps them to believe that the negative behaviors experienced as a child will never happen again.

When you understand your mate, you will continue to build their self-esteem regardless of their hair. Our mates are the way they are because of what they have been through. We have all been through difficult times within our lives. Some have been through great times and want those times to continue regardless of who they are with. When you understand your mate, you will see why some people would rather be involved with someone who has money instead of someone who does not.

"I am going to get my hair done and I don't care what you say"?

Based on understanding your mate, you will also discover why Hollywood stars are struggling in their relationships. Please do not forget that money is an enhancer of who you are and what you enjoy doing. Please do not forget the individual in the relationship regardless of the money or the occupation. Everyone wants to be with someone who loves and understands them. **When you understand your mate, you will have found the key to true and pure love. Have you ever heard someone say, "It's my money. I'll spend it how I want to"?** Many people will call a person who says this controlling, but remember if they are controlling, there is a reason.

MONEY ISSUES

Seeking to understand will help you discover why this person wants things their way when it comes to financial matters. Perhaps they have always been rich, and they noticed that people have used them for their money. This person has decided they are not going to allow anyone to use them for their money again. No one wants to play the role of a fool. When you understand this person, you may discover that trust is an issue. If trust in an issue, then you realize that you have to get this person to trust you. Therefore, the question would be, "Are you trustworthy?" I love understanding your mate because it keeps the relationship fresh. It feels like I am forever dating my wife.

When you understand your mate, you will continue to build their self-esteem regardless of their hair.

Through every financial decision we make, we are always trying to understand why she or I chose one decision over another. I was the kind of husband who would not give money toward grocery shopping, but I would give money to friends and strangers so that they could go grocery shopping. Okay, before you all judge me, seek to understand. Why would I, a husband, give money to others, but not to my family? What would you imagine my reasoning would be

When you understand your mate, you will have found the key to true and pure love. Have you ever heard someone say, "It's my money. I'll spend it how I want to"?

for such a decision? I am not going to give you the answer; I just want you to begin the process of seeking to understand. I will tell you that once my wife understood me, she was able to get me to spend more money at home and less money outside of our home. My wife does everything for the home and nothing outside of the house. Can you forecast our money issues?

KEY 18
SELF COUNSELING

If you were the counselor, would you tell her or me what to do, or would you seek to understand why we function in such a way? If you are the kind of counselor who would tell me to stop spending outside the house without understanding me, you would lose. If you would tell my wife to start helping others more without understanding her, you would lose. Our marriage would still be in trouble after leaving your office. Why? People do not change their behaviors because a counselor told them to do so. People change behaviors because they see a need to change or because someone who understands them has given them helpful information that makes change seem right.

Therefore, the change must be willing and not forced. Counselors who do not counsel from an understanding perspective leave couples in the same state. This is why couples still divorce after seeing a counselor. Too often counselors do not know how to better relationships. A counselor should never chose sides. The relationship is owned by the two individuals. When a counselor provides faults, the relationship is in more trouble because people do not want to feel attacked. This is one reason why men do not attend church. Most relationship messages in church attack men in front of women. Understanding your mate changes the focus from faults to solutions.

> Some people do not want a divorce and their last hope is a counselor.

Understanding your mate provides a new perspective on counseling. **Some people do not want a divorce and their last hope is a counselor.** When they leave the counselor's office, however, they file for divorce. I went to a counselor who told me to divorce my wife. The counselor believed that I wanted to divorce and just needed someone to tell me to do so. I thank God that I did not listen. My wife and I have a new relationship because of understanding your mate. Like many others, our relationship had thousands of issues, but understanding your mate has caused every issue to be a stepping-stone to a better and closer relationship. Finally, I am in a long-lasting, happy relationship, thanks to understanding your mate.

KEY 19

FROM THE DATING TO THE "I DO" MARRIAGE

Notice what happens when you move from dating to marriage. This is where the real "fun" begins. Whenever you hear people say that there has been a change since the marriage, they are saying that something is different. Many people believe that there is no difference between marriage and living with someone. Some people who have lived together unmarried for twenty years notice a great change in their relationship when they marry. However, I disagree because there is a difference. The difference is not physical; it is psychological. I call this difference, "Humans vs. Robots."

During dating, people are human. Humans are funny and have a sense of humor. Humans lie for the sake of not hurting someone. I didn't say that I agree.

I am just talking about the behaviors of humans. **Let's be honest: humans are freaky.** Humans are polite; they open doors and help put coats on others. Robots, on the other hand, do what they are told. **Robots do what they are programmed to do.** Robots have no feelings. When they speak, they have no thought. They just speak. If someone gets hurt, oh well. Robots do not eat nor do they care about others' feelings. Robots represent many couples in marriage.

Couples get married and all of a sudden, they change their human nature. **The question that is unconsciously asked is, "How did I become a robot?"** People become robots by moving into their ideologies on what they believe marriage should be. Fear becomes a great part of their lives. People become afraid of divorce, afraid of losing so-called friends, afraid of changing, and therefore robotedness kicks in. Whenever you stop being the person your mate married, you are moving into a robotic situation. It is true that some things will change. **Change is a part of the relationship.**

You do not lose anything when you change; you only add to the fruitfulness of your life. You cannot continue being a player of you played on your mate. However, you should continue to be a player with your mate. If you were silly before the wedding, continue the silliness after the wedding. Many people say that it is time to grow up, but you cannot grow up to the marriage, you grow up with your mate and the marriage. **In your ideology, you thought that being a robot was the right way.** How many people get married and assume the behaviors they think they should implement in their lives because they have gotten married? This is a mistake for so many new marriages. It is this ideology that leads people to want out of the relationship because they feel too much pressure. This pressure, however, is self-inflicted.

> Change is a part of the relationship.

Whenever you try to be the best mate that you can be based on a textbook, then you are in trouble. You want to be the best mate for and according to your mate, not a mate in a book, movie, and/or television series. **Robots do not share their feelings openly. They tend to complain in secret.** They are frustrated and it shows in their behaviors although they may not say anything to their mate. Understanding your mate will stop you from becoming a robot. Understanding your mate will keep you in the dating scene with your mate although you are now married. When you seek to understand your mate, you experience laughter and good times. Many times couples do not have much to talk about. Understanding your mate gives you a lot to talk about. Understanding your mate creates a positive atmosphere for great communication.

KEY 20

COMMUNICATION DISTORTION

This leads to the last chapter in understanding your mate: "Communication Distortion." *Not all men or all women communicate in the same way.* A man or woman who finds it difficult to verbally share their feelings has a reason for this difficulty. The person may be afraid of how their feelings will be interpreted. Experience may have taught them that whenever they verbally express themselves, people respond negatively toward them. Some people have learned to survive by remaining quiet. Past relationships may have been abusive and the reason given was their verbal expressions. Understand why your mate finds it difficult to share without judging them by understanding their experiences. People are different and unique. They have unique experiences, they have the problem resolved, another problem emerges.

Sometimes mates feel as though they cannot please the other mate. This occurs because one mate is constantly complaining, and the mate who is hearing the complaint does not know how to resolve the real issue. Remember if a mate is complaining, they are complaining for a reason. Understanding your mate will give you access to the real issue and the tools to solve the main problem.

Not all men or all women communicate in the same way.

In too many cases, the smallest issue leads to the biggest battle. This is because the small issue was not the main issue. The small issue was simply used to create an avenue for the main issue to be expressed. Many relationships take each other's complaint at face value. **It is never face value.** It is important for you to ask about the real problem. Sometimes the real problem might be that a person found out that they owe money that they do not have. It may be a conversation they had earlier with their baby's mother or father. Finding out the real issue will allow you and your mate to resolve the issue and move forward to more happy times.

The main problem with communication is being

misunderstood or your mate misinterpreting your words. In the book, *Interpersonal Communication: Relating to Others,* by Beebe, Beebe, and Remond, it states that it is still possible to misunderstand the speaker because of self-issues and concerns. This is why it is critically important to seek first to understand, and then be understood. When you seek first to be understood, it leaves you to misinterpret the message that is being communicated by your mate. A good exercise would be for you to tell your mate that you saw an old friend and notice if your mate interprets that you are saying you wished you were with them.

> **It is never face value.**

If your mate interprets that you wish you were them, your mate is seeking to be understood, and not seeking to understand At the same time, your mate may have misinterpreted your message because they have been cheated on in the past. Remember, your mate has a reason for interpreting the wrong message. Your mate may have fears and insecurities within the relationship. Some people assume that because a person has insecurities within the relationship, the person is insecure. This is not true. It is very possible to have insecurities within a relationship and be a secure person.

When you understand your mate, you will discover that sometimes there are behaviors that are going on in the relationship that are making your mate insecure. For example, if your mate was on the phone until 2 a.m. with someone of the opposite sex, would it make you insecure about the relationship? If you are excited about someone else and not about your mate, it can cause your mate to feel insecure. This behavior also leads to misinterpretation within the communication process. When speaking to your mate, remember to whom you are speaking. Often, we speak to our mates as if we are speaking to ourselves. When you share information, you must be considerate to your mate.

> **The main problem with communication is being misunderstood or your mate misinterpreting your words.**

KEY 21

COMMUNICATION DISTORTION *PART 2*

The way we communicate can create communication distortion. *Hollering at your mate may not work, and speaking softly to your mate may not work.* Understanding your mate will teach you the proper way to communicate with them—it will teach you a way that will work. You cannot communicate with your mate the way you want them to communicate with you. Dr. Beebe states that, "Communication styles also fit the receiver, not just the messenger." You have to communicate with your mate so that they can hear you. Understanding your mate teaches you how your mate wants you to communicate with them. If your mate is used to abusive people hollering at them, when you holler, they may conclude that you are going to be abusive or full of drama. People respond to different styles of communication for various reasons.

Your mate may regard soft speaking as a sign of weakness because of their experiences. ***Everyone is different.*** Everyone communicates in their own way. The key is to understand how your mate communicates. When speaking to your mate, learn how to respond to their communication style. It is also important to treat your mate the way they are and not the way you are. You may be able to handle loud tones, but your mate may consider loud tones abusive. Understanding your mate gives you the keys to unlock your mate's communication style.

> **Hollering at your mate may not work, and speaking softly to your mate may not work.**

KEY 22

COMMUNICATION DISTORTION *PART 3*

While some people do not verbalize their feelings for many reasons, others do verbalize their feelings. The reason that some people are very verbal could be the same reason that others are not. ***Some mates may verbalize their thoughts because they were hurt when they did not do this in the past.*** Others had their quietness used against them and vowed that they would never keep quiet. ***Some mates speak up because they do not want to appear soft or cowardly.*** This is why it is vital to understand your mate. When you understand your mate, you learn how they are and why they are this way.

It is unfortunate, but the truth is old relationships have shaped and molded individuals for their new relationships. This molding can be either positive or negative. For example, if my last mate lied to me several times, it is going to be difficult for me to believe my new mate is telling the truth. My last mate created a mindset that I didn't have prior to being with her. If my new mate does not understand me, however, then the relationship is going to have some serious obstacles.

> **Some mates may verbalize their thoughts because they were hurt when they did not do this in the past.**

Understanding your mate is truly the key to a lasting, happy relationship. Understanding your mate provides the tools necessary for love, excellent communication, fantastic sex, solutions for money concerns, and getting rid of myths and ideology.

SUMMATION

Love is a creative process and the process must never end. With new situations, we need continual love. This love occurs with understanding your mate. The inability to communicate has been a root cause of broken relationships. Understanding your mate will teach you how to communicate with your mate. The communication will be effective and joyful.

Sex is a must in marriage. A marriage cannot survive without sex. Sex does not have to be intercourse. There are other ways to please one another sexually. Understanding your mate will teach you how to please your mate. Sex will not get rid of relationship issues, but it will give you the relaxation of the mind needed to handle any issue that arises. Research has taught us that money is the number-one reason why a couple might divorce.

Understanding your mate will reveal to you how and why your mate feels a certain way about money. Understanding their thoughts and reasons will provide the tools to create an understanding with the relationship that will be helpful to the relationship. The negotiations will operate smoothly when you understand your mate.

The myths and ideology of marriage and relationships starts the breakup before the relationship begins. Myths are only great if you plan to remain single, but if you are planning and hoping to marry, your ideology will not work. Understanding your mate will create a philosophy for the relationship that is agreed upon by both parties. The relationship cannot be one-sided, and understanding your mate will provide the balance that is necessary for a lasting and happy union.

Rev. Antonio Harlan

One reason causes all relationship failures
Understanding universal key to healing relationships

There is only one reason why relationships fail. Rev. Antonio Harlan, healing relationship counselor of more than 10 years, knows from experience and practice. He says understanding cures all relationships. The respected relationship counselor shares this healing key with individuals and couples in his practice and congregation. He created **Understanding Your Mate,** a four CD series with stand alone workbook as a result of his personal experience and practice. The Detroit native details the underlying causes of relationship failure and teaches listeners to heal their relationships through understanding and customization.

God honors Marriage. **As Understanding Your Mate** explodes all over the world, partners are experiencing long hoped for happiness in their marriages. Rev. Harlan continues to experience God's honor of his marriage as he walks his talk. When his marriage was threatened with divorce, Rev. Harlan received a clear message from God. He told him how to rescue his and other marriages to drive the rapidly escalating divorce rates down.

Understanding Your Mate True Key to Relationship Happiness

Contrary to popular reports that claim compatibility as the key to lasting, happy relationships; Rev. Harlan explains the **true** key to creating relationship success– *understanding your mate.* Compatibility occurs when two people agree with certain behaviors, says Rev. Harlan. They may be like-minded and friendly towards each other. Knowledge changes as the relationship changes. Unless that knowledge comes with the perception that leads to understanding, partners compatible today can find themselves no longer partners or even compatible in five years. When those same individuals seek to understand one another, then each finds themselves understood, while developing an even better self understanding.

Understanding Your Mate Wins Them Heart and Soul

When you understand your mate, you win them heart and soul, Rev. Harlan reveals. Everyone wants to be with someone who regards their unique and unusual individuality with understanding. What makes your mate happy? And why does *that* make them happy. During counseling sessions, (live or via CD) Rev. Harlan helps mates understand each other as they learn the distinctive aspects of their relationship. Once they see that they have misread or misunderstood their mate, the understanding revelation renews the relationship and a new lasting union forms. Compassion, acceptance of each other's differences, acceptance of each other's weaknesses and strengths, patience, tolerance, charity and love fills the revitalized association.

Understanding Makes Forgiveness and Compassion Possible in Love Process

The creative course of action called love requires work, says Rev. Harlan. First, we choose to love with the understanding that loving means action. *Understanding Your Mate* creates an environment where real love happens. With love grows compassion and forgiveness. The constant thought process of understanding your mate stops partners from judging and allows each to accept the other's differences. Understanding our mates forces us to regard them with compassion. *"I love you"* becomes more than mere words spoken after knowing someone. With understanding *"I love you"* expresses a plan of action and intention.

For more information on Rev. Antonio Harlan, booksignings, speaking engagements, or to order additional copies of this book or his other motivational materials, contact:

AMZA Publishing
16250 Northland Dr., Suite 210
Southfield, MI 48075
Tel: 313.632.6527
E:Mail: amza@comcast.net
www.understandingyourmate.com